Santa's Stormy Christmas Eve

Written by David MacLennan
Illustrated by Cheryl Parkinson

Full Satchel Press

To: Odessa,
Merry Christmas (2006)
Dave (Mac Lennan)

It was now Christmas Eve and Santa couldn't believe

that he'd ever seen weather as foul;

And at sixty below, in a swirl of thick snow,

the north wind filled the skies with a howl.

With their arms 'round themselves, the cold, weary elves,

chattered hard in their thin suits of green;

And while chilled to his gizzard, Santa said, "This bad blizzard

just might be the worst that I've seen."

Tucked away in the stable Santa sat at a table,

    surrounded by all his reindeer;

And as the hour to fly very quickly drew nigh,

    his face became etched with great fear.

Neatly stacked by the sleigh all the brand new toys lay,

    as old Santa still studied the storm;

And oh, what a sad sight, Rudolph's nose wouldn't light,

    as he crept to the fire to get warm.

Then a sense of great doom flooded into the room,

  as the reindeer pawed hard at the floor;

And their fears were well founded, for they could be grounded,

  by the winds that continued to roar.

It was such a nightmare and it seemed so unfair

  that the weather could keep them at bay;

Just the thought of sad faces, in so many places,

  of the children on this Christmas Day...

What a terrible state! What a wretched, cruel fate!

  Now, whatever could dear Santa do?

Yes, it all was so tragic, not even his magic

  could change this bad weather, he knew.

He envisioned the worst, would this year be the first,

  there'd be nothing to write in his log?

And with spirits a-sinking, he found himself thinking

  of Rudolph and the Christmas of fog.

But that was so long ago, now the problem was snow;

    oh, so heavy, and blinding, and white.

Then at last Santa stood and he pulled on his hood,

    and he trundled out into the night.

"Come along my wee elves, let us bundle ourselves;

    together we'll give it a try."

So, upon these brave words his good helpers all stirred,

    and burst forth with a determined cry!

Now, with toys in the sleigh there was no more to say,

    as the elves held the team good and steady,

And despite bitter cold the reindeer stood bold,

    braced into the wind - they were ready.

Santa clambered aboard, while the mighty wind roared,

    and the snow churned about in the blow;

Then, he took up the reins, as the elves cleared the lanes,

    and with a whoop, he cried out, "High-thee-ho!"

But, so tough was their luck that the sleigh became stuck,

from the deep ruts it couldn't be budged;

And so, out of the storm to the stable so warm,

Santa, reindeer and elves sadly trudged.

When he threw back his hood, they then understood

their predicament's terrible cost.

Mother Nature's harsh trick, here played on St. Nick -

could the spirit of Christmas be lost?

Now, sunk deep in his chair, it all seemed so unfair,

    Santa stared away off into space;

And the expression of pain, was engraved to remain

    on his usually jovial face.

Nothing more could he do, he unhappily knew,

    he'd lost to the wretched great freeze;

"For tonight," Santa sighed, "not a toy can I hide,

    under each of the good children's trees."

Oh, so glum were the elves, putting toys on the shelves,

    saddened by their despicable plight;

When, lo and behold, stepping in from the cold,

    came a man from the dark, stormy night.

Dressed in white summer clothes, one could only suppose

    why his nose and his toes were not froze;

But, he was a warm sight, bathed in soft glowing light,

    as he entered the stable of woes.

And it seemed the dark gloom that had flooded the room,

    disappeared and the air became clear;

Yes, there was a new lease, with an aura of peace,

    that helped lift the great burden of fear.

Now, St. Nick, fully aware, leaping out of his chair,

    adjusting his specs as he stood,

Beheld this tall man with a book in his hand

    and his face, oh, so kind and so good.

Then in soft gentle tone, with compassion shown,

    the tall stranger with tenderness spoke;

"Well, my dear Santa Claus, whom we love without pause,

    and a hero to all the young folk -

Let me first make it clear why I have come here,

    to the cold and stormy North Pole;

It's from Heaven above, with a heart full of love,

    that I've come to help with your goal.

"I'm the Messenger Sent, and my mission is meant

    to show you what we can achieve;

For in dreams we can fly, if we truly try,

    and in miracles we all believe.

So, dear Santa and elves, let us gather ourselves

    and into the storm we will go;

For the hour grows late, while the good children wait,

    and time is a-wasting you know."

So, just as before, they burst out of the door,

   scrambling to the sleigh to grab hold;

And with a hand lent, from the Messenger Sent,

   they pushed into the wind and the cold.

Yet, unlike before, there was something much more,

   and a far greater power they found;

For, with one mighty heave, they could hardly believe

   how quickly the sleigh left the ground.

Now, up went a cheer that the whole world could hear,

　　as Santa flew into the sky;

And with praises to sing the Messenger took wing,

　　with these parting words of goodbye:

"To love and to share are the best gifts you bear,

　　dear Santa, in your shiny red sleigh;

And as onward you go, please tell the children below,

　　the true meaning of this joyous day."

Peace, goodwill and a Merry Christmas to all.

First edition 2003   Full Satchel Press is registered in Canada.

National Library of Canada Cataloguing in Publication Data

MacLennan, David, 1950-
Santa's Stormy Christmas Eve / written by David MacLennan ; illustrated by Cheryl Parkinson.

ISBN 0-9731960-0-9

1. Christmas stories, Canadian (English)* 2. Santa Claus--Juvenile fiction. I. Parkinson, Cheryl, 1946- II. Title.
PS8575.L458S26 2003   jC813'.6   C2003-910338-2
PZ7.M22493Sa 2003

To my parents, Jean and Rod, and my nephews, Shawn and Steven Matthias.
- Dave

To my parents, Doris and Paul, The Temiskaming Pallette and Brush Club and Carolyn and Laura at Canvas and Clay.
- Cheryl

With special thanks and gratitude, to Vivian Amy Bruce, whose brilliant editing has made this book possible.

Hands-On Design, Art Direction by Carol E. Hyland, Victoria, British Columbia Canada.

The illustrations in this book were done in a process called ink resist and using mixed media.